Ripley Goes to School

TRACY SCHLEPPHORST
ART BY DIPESH SHAH

www.EmotionBellyBooks.com

In memory of the dogs who loved me unconditionally through the years: Trouble, Monty, Shadow, Sheba, Fancy, and Mia. To Ripley for providing the inspiration for this book and approaching life with nothing but love. To Poppy, the puppy, for teaching me patience as you grow.

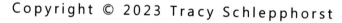

We can learn a lot about how a dog feels by the position of their tail. Can you name the doggy emotion of each tail?

Ripley was so excited that her whole body wiggled! It was a school visit day!

She dashed out of the house
and into the car!

Ripley sniffed the fresh air as she zipped and zoomed down the road.

Finally, she spotted the school up ahead. Ripley could hardly wait to meet her new friends.

Everyone smiled as she walked into the building.

Ripley smiled back by wagging her tail.

She stepped into the classroom and her nose started twitching as the familiar smells of erasers, crayons, and stinky socks wafted through the air.

Her tail wagged again. Those smells always meant a full day of making kids happy. And making kids happy made Ripley feel happy.

She carefully investigated the group of faces.

In the corner of the room, Ripley noticed a few students moving closer to the teacher. Their nervous eyes met with hers. Ripley knew how it felt to be nervous – to be scared. She felt that way the first time she visited a school.

Ripley gently walked into the group. The children were taking turns touching her soft fur.

She couldn't help but sniff the shoes of students with familiar dog smells. Ripley loved other dogs and was curious about the smells.

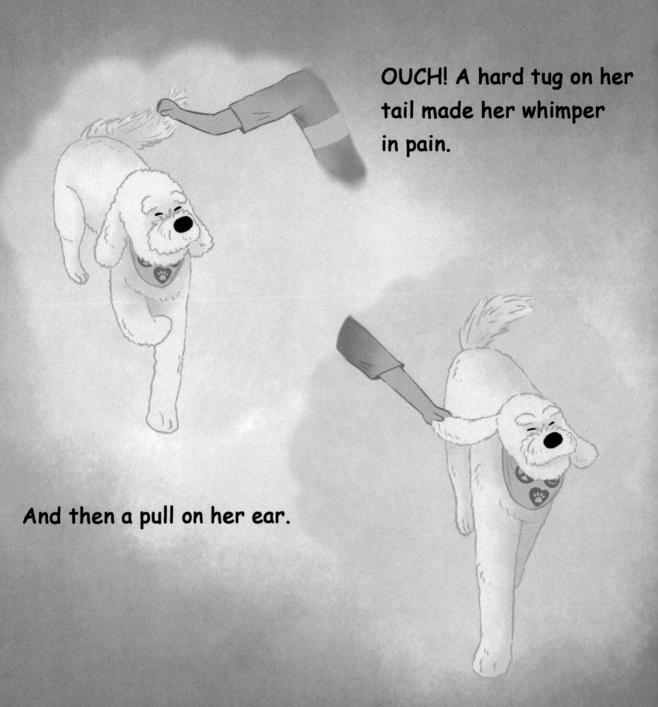

OUCH! A hard tug on her tail made her whimper in pain.

And then a pull on her ear.

Ripley jumped away from the children. She hung her head and tucked her tail. Why would someone treat her this way?

"Henry," cried a little girl, "you can't treat dogs like that! You need to use your manners!"

Henry raised his hand, "I'm sorry I pulled Ripley's tail and her ear. I didn't mean to hurt her. May I please have another chance to pet her nicely?"

Ripley watched carefully as Henry walked toward her. She wondered if he would hurt her again.

She waited as he got down on the ground by her.
He reached out his hand and gently petted her fur.

"I'm sorry Ripley." Henry whispered,
"I promise I won't do it again."

Ripley licked Henry's face. This felt a lot better!

But Ripley was a little more cautious now as she made her way around to the rest of the kids. She knew she would get away quickly if anyone else ever tried to hurt her.

Ripley still had a few tricks left to share.
Everyone clapped and laughed as she twirled
and danced around.

"Ripley, you're a rockstar!" shouted Henry.

When their time was up, Ripley walked through the group for one last pat and hug.

The kids didn't want her to leave!

She wagged her tail and held her head up high, as she walked down the hall to the next classroom.

Ripley glanced back over her shoulder and all the students were waving good-bye to her.

"We love you, Ripley!" Henry exclaimed.

WE WOULD LOVE TO HAVE YOU TO FOLLOW US ON
Facebook.com/emotionbellybooks
Instagram: @doodle.wonder

ALSO BY THIS AUTHOR:

Tracy Schlepphorst is the founder of Emotion Belly Books, a book series designed to help children better understand their emotions. Tracy's book series includes: Eden and Her Happy, Henry and His Manners, Eden and Her Joy, Ripley Wonders About Books, and My Emotional Belly. Along with her love of writing she enjoys sharing her stories in classrooms and speaking at live events. Tracy also enjoys spending time outside, tennis, golf, biking, and paddleboarding.

Tracy's greatest joy is spending time with her family: John, Aly, Walker, Melanie, Sam, and Emma. And of course Ripley and Poppy, at home in Quincy, Illinois.

You can learn more about Tracy on both

Facebook: Tracy Schlepphorst– Emotion Belly Books
& Instagram: @doodle.wonder

I've always been an artist; it's in my blood!
I reside in India, and I am extremely grateful to be able to contribute my artwork to children's books that benefit both the younger generation and adults. I am blessed with great parents who supported me in every decision of my life. I'd like to thank Tracy for providing me with several chances and for her unwavering belief in me. You're the best Tracy!

My art page on Instagram-
www.instagram.com/artbydipesh

Made in the USA
Las Vegas, NV
16 October 2023

79214404R10021